Shoo Rayner

ROMAN
BRIT

BALLISTIC LOGISTIC

ORCHARD BOOKS
338 Euston Road, London NW1 3BH
Orchard Books Australia
Level 17/207 Kent Street, Sydney, NSW 2000

First published in 2015 by Orchard Books
ISBN 978 1 40833 449 2

A CIP catalogue record for this book is available
from the British Library.

1 3 5 7 9 10 8 6 4 2

Printed in Great Britain

Orchard Books is an imprint of Hachette Children's Group
and published by The Watts Publishing Group Limited, an Hachette UK company.

www.hachette.co.uk

Shoo Rayner

ROMAN
BRIT

BALLISTIC LOGISTIC

ORCHARD

FORT FINIS TERRAE is a sleepy backwater in the great Roman Empire. A young shepherd boy named Brit lives there with his sheep and faithful dog Festus.

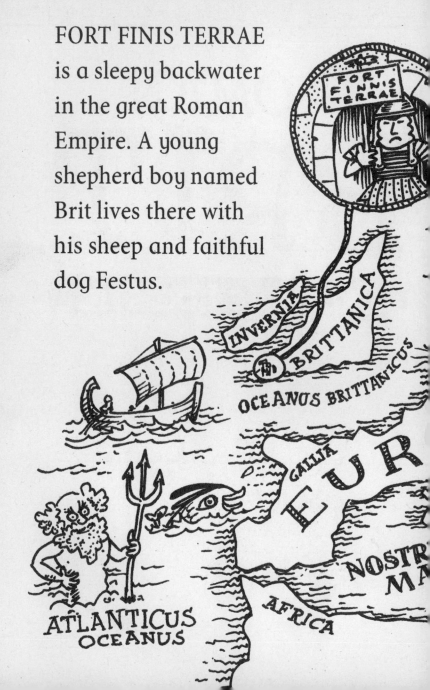

It's a quiet life for Brit and his animals in the fort. But every so often, something happens to make it a day to remember!

GERMANIA

A

ARABIA

CHAPTER ONE

"By Jupiter, Janus and Jove! What was that?"

Brit leapt out of bed and froze as an enormous bang brought a rafter crashing down where he had been dozing just moments before.

Festus barked at the ceiling. The sheep at the doorway scattered in all directions. Chickens clucked and flapped, leaving feathers floating in the air.

"Stop!" Brit yelled at the top of his voice.

After a moment's silence, a voice shouted from outside. "Is someone in there?"

"Yes," Brit called. "Me!"

"Who's me?"

"Brit!"

"Brit? What are you doing in there?"

"I live here!" Brit yelled.

Shadows blocked the early morning
sun that poured through the doorway. A
dozen Roman soldiers peered in at Brit.

Their leader, Chief Engineer Bumptius
Matius, stepped forward.

"But you can't live here," Bumptius insisted. "We're building a road, and it's coming right through here!" With a sweep of his hand, he indicated a line through the centre of Brit's barn. Brit stared at him in horror.

"But... but... this is my home!"

CHAPTER TWO

The day had started out so well. For the
last few weeks, Brit had been working hard,
helping with the harvest. He had filled his
barn with hay, barley, cabbages and turnips
– enough to keep his animals fed over the
winter.

Brit loved his barn. It wasn't much – the
walls were made from piled-up river stones
and the roof was made of pine saplings
covered in thatch. But it was
his own little world – a world that was
falling down around him in clouds of dust
and spiderwebs.

Brit looked sadly around at the destruction
of his home. A girl's voice pierced the air.

"What are you doing to Brit's barn?"

Oh no! Brit thought to himself.
Drusilla!

Drusilla was the daughter of Gluteus
Maximus, the Commander of Fort Finis
Terrae. She didn't have any friends of
her own, so she had to make do with
Brit. She thought of him as a kind of pet
that needed
looking after.

"She's
going to
make a bad
day even
worse," Brit
whispered
to Festus.

"What are you doing?" Drusilla demanded again. The soldiers all jumped to attention when she spoke.

"We've got orders, Miss," Bumptius explained. "We've got to build a road so we can bring the catapult through here for firing practice."

"Don't be silly!" Drusilla sighed. She addressed the soldiers as if they were small children. "You can just build the road to go around the barn."

The men gasped and looked at each other in shock.

"But we are soldiers of the Roman Army, Miss!" one said.

"Our roads always go straight, straight, straight!" said another.

"We don't go around things. Nothing stands in the way of the Roman Army!"

Bumptius nodded in agreement. "Let me show you something," he said to the children, leading them to an odd-looking device. "This is a *goma*."

Five strings dangled from a cross that was attached to the top of a pole.

"These strings are plumb lines," he explained. "This middle one is set directly over a marker in the middle of the road."

"Where are the plums?" Brit asked. He'd been picking plums in the orchard the day before.

Not that kind of plum," Bumptius laughed. "A plumb line is a string with a weight on the end. The weight always keeps the string vertical. That's how we build things straight."

"That's clever," Drusilla smiled.

"First you line up two of the outer strings and the middle string with the road you've built already, like this." Bumptius showed how the *goma* was lined up with the road from the fort.

"When you look from the other direction," he continued, "you'll see that the strings line up on Brit's barn. Orders are orders, Miss. That's where the road has to go! Straight, straight, straight!"

Drusilla folded her arms and furrowed her forehead. "Oh, this is ridiculous," she snorted. "I'm going to see my daddy and sort this out right now! Nobody do anything until I return." She turned on her heels and marched back down the road to the fort.

Brit and Bumptius looked at each other and shrugged their shoulders.

Brit sighed. Drusilla's way of sorting things out was not always how he would choose to do things. He also knew that nothing would stop the Roman Army when it had made its mind up to do something.

The soldiers sat on their battering ram and waited. Drusilla was the Fort Commander's daughter. Was it possible she could get the Roman Army to change its mind?

In the distance they heard the squeak of wooden wheels and the sound of soldiers chanting as they hauled the giant catapult along the road.

"Unus, Duo, Tres, Quattuor,
We are Roman men of war.
If anyone gets in our way,
We'll bash them down and
make them pay!"

Gluteus Maximus, the Fort Commander, was striding towards Brit, ahead of his men. He'd come to see exactly what the problem was. Drusilla followed him, tugging at the skirts of his tunic.

"Really, Daddy!" she said crossly. "Can't you just make the road go around Brit's barn?"

Gluteus stopped and stared at his daughter in surprise.

"My dear," he said, very slowly, as if he thought Drusilla might not understand.

 "We are the Roman Army. Our roads always go straight, straight, straight! We don't go around things. Nothing stands in our way!"

He gazed kindly at his darling, simple daughter, and showed her the map that was drawn of a piece of tree bark.

"It's quite straightforward, my dear. The road comes out of the fort and goes straight to the top of the hill, where we are setting up the new catapult firing range. It's all here on the plan."

"Begging your pardon, Sir," Brit piped up, bowing his head so he didn't have to look into the Commander's fierce eyes. "But what about my barn?"

Gluteus sighed. "The barn is not on this plan, so it doesn't matter. And anyway, I'm the Commander of the Fort, and everything else around here, as far as the eye can see. So it's *my* barn, and I'll do what I like with it."

"But Brit lives there!" Drusilla pleaded.

Gluteus Maximus sighed again, more loudly, and scanned the countryside.

"He can live there!" he said, pointing further down the valley, where a tumbled-down shack was doing its best to stay upright.

"Come along!" Gluteus shouted orders at the soldiers. "Let's get this road built!"

As the soldiers got back to work, Drusilla stood open-mouthed in shock. She could usually make her dad do anything, but when he was being a soldier, it was like he became another person – someone who just wouldn't do as he was told.

Brit ran up to the Commander and coughed nervously. "Excuse me, Sir, but what about my sheep, and all their food I've stored for the winter inside the barn?"

Gluteus Maximus looked down at Brit as if he wasn't on the plan either. "They're *my* sheep," he snapped. "You just look after them."

"Oh yes, Sir. But excuse me, Sir. What are *your* sheep going to eat over the winter?"

Gluteus Maximus considered the problem for a moment. Then turned to Bumptius Matius.

"Help the boy clear the barn!" he barked. "Then get it knocked down as quickly as possible, or you'll all be on sentry duty for a month. Nothing stands in the way of the Roman Army!"

CHAPTER THREE

Not long after, the few things that
Brit owned had been piled outside his
barn, along with all the food he had so
carefully harvested for the winter.

The soldiers picked up the battering
ram again and charged at the barn.

BANG! BANG! BANG!

Again and again they charged, until only a pile of stone and timber lay where Brit's cosy home had once stood.

Drusilla walked over to Brit and picked up one of his turnips. "Come along, Brit," she said cheerily. "Let's get all this stuff moved to your new barn."

Drusilla had clearly decided that if she couldn't sort her father out, she would have to sort Brit out instead.

"One turnip at a time?" Brit muttered under his breath. "That will take till the next harvest."

Brit harnessed Festus into a small, two-wheeled cart and loaded it with hay. He piled more bundles of hay onto his shoulders, and began moving his precious harvest to the new barn.

"That's the way to do it!" Drusilla trilled as she passed him on her way back for another turnip. "A few more trips and we'll soon be done!"

"You must be out of your tiny mi...!"

But Brit's voice was drowned out by the heaving and harrumphing of the soldiers, who had dragged the mighty catapult right through where his barn had been. Now they were positioning the huge machine, getting it ready to fire.

"Right, men," said Gluteus Maximus, "This is the new catapult training range."

"What stones should we use for ammunition, Sir?" asked Bumptius Matius.

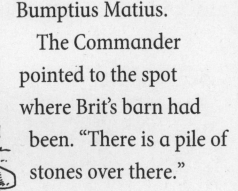

The Commander pointed to the spot where Brit's barn had been. "There is a pile of stones over there."

"And what's the target, Sir?" Bumptius Matius asked.

Gluteus Maximus narrowed his eyes and surveyed the countryside. He pointed further down the valley. "See that flock of sheep? If you can hit one of them, then it's mutton stew for supper tonight."

"Mutton stew!" Brit gulped. "But... that means... my sheep!" he wailed.

"Er... *My* sheep, I think you mean?" Gluteus Maximus smiled thinly.

The men sang as they winched down the arm of the catapult.

♪ *"Unus, Duo, Tres, Quattuor,*
We are Roman men of war. ♪
If we get our aim just right, ♪
♪ *We'll have mutton stew tonight!"*

Gluteus Maximus raised his arm as a signal. "Aim and... fire!"

With a loud clang and a giant twang, the catapult sent an enormous rock flying through the air.

Unaware of the danger hurtling towards them, the sheep carried on eating and *baa*-ing as if the world couldn't have been a better or happier place. Everyone held their breath.

THUD!

The rock ploughed into the soft earth just a few arms' lengths short of the target. The sheep lifted their heads, looked around for a moment or two, then carried on eating as if nothing had happened.

The second rock landed closer, just a lamb's tail away.

Brit whistled a command that only Festus could understand. The whistle meant: *Festus, get our sheep out of there!*

Festus knew his job. The hound raced down the hill with the little cart rattling and bumping along behind him. He yapped and barked, telling the sheep to get out of there as quickly as possible.

The soldiers were making the catapult ready again.

"Aim and… fire!" Gluteus Maximus ordered.

The second rock flew through the air. Brit realised with horror that Festus was right in its path!

"Phweeee!"

Brit whistled a warning. He covered his eyes and squinted through the cracks in his fingers. The whistle echoed round and round the valley.

The rock crashed into the back of the dog cart. Splinters of wood flew in all directions. Festus, relieved of the load, tumbled over a few times, and lay still.

Brit held his breath. Drusilla looked like she was about to cry.

But after a few very long seconds,
the hound began to stir. Brit felt relief
wash over him as Festus picked himself
up, barked to say he was all right and
headed back towards the sheep.

Gluteus Maximus shouted at his men.
"You dozy nincompoops! You couldn't
hit a wall if it was right in front of you.
Come along, quick fire! We've got a
moving target now!"

The panicked sheep scattered in all directions. It was bad enough that Festus was chasing them, but now, whichever way they turned, rocks were pouring out of the sky as well. Festus raced around them in circles, barking himself hoarse.

"Swing it round this way!" Gluteus Maximus yelled at his men. "And... fire!"

Brit whistled secret signals to Festus, telling him which way to go.

After a few minutes, the dog had the sheep gathered together in a tight bunch. Brit blasted one, long, loud, clear whistle. Festus knew what it meant. *Run for it!*

As rock after rock thudded into the soft turf, Festus drove the sheep across the valley and far away into the distance.

"Idiots!" Gluteus Maximus growled at his men. "Never mind mutton stew, there'll be no supper at all tonight, and sentry duties for the next six months! You've let yourselves down, you've let me down and you've let the whole Roman Army down. I hope you are ashamed of yourselves."

He glowered at Bumptius Matius. "I'm leaving you in charge. If you can't get them to hit a target by the end of the day, you'll be peeling turnips for the rest of your life!"

Gluteus turned smartly on his heels and marched off, back to the fort.

As the soldiers wearily began practising again, they sang a slow, mournful dirge.

♫ *"Unus, Duo, Tres, Quattuor,* ♪
We don't want to fight no more.
♪ *Get the target in the sight,* ♪
Or we're not going to eat tonight!"

Brit sat down on the ground, feeling thoroughly miserable. His beloved barn had been demolished and bits of it were scattered all over the valley. His harvest was dumped in a huge pile and he had no way to carry it to the new barn, which needed rebuilding anyway.

He put the few things he owned into his big cooking pot. Then he filled it to the top with turnips and cabbages. It was far too heavy to carry on his own.

The soldiers just sat and watched. No one offered to help. They all blamed Brit for chasing the sheep away. That's why they weren't getting any supper tonight.

Brit dragged the pot down to the new barn. When he arrived, his heart sank even further. It was just a shack. The walls were falling in and the roof had holes in it. The rocks and stones that his old barn had been made of lay scattered all around it.

Brit scowled at the giant catapult. But then he remembered how the huge machine had effortlessly hurled those rocks about. Slowly, an idea began to form in his mind, and he felt a faint glimmer of hope.

"Let's get cooking," he said, making sparks with his flint so he could get a fire going.

"Will that help?" asked Drusilla, who had just delivered yet another turnip.

Brit nodded at the grumpy-looking soldiers and smiled. "It will make them feel even more hungry. They'll do anything for food."

As he chopped up turnips and put them in the pot, he explained his plan. Drusilla smiled. There was a job to do, and she was the girl to do it!

She ran back over to the men. "Listen up!" she ordered. "Brit is cooking a load of food. Does anyone want to share it?"

The delicious smell of cooking wafted under the hungry soldiers' noses. They all got up and scrambled towards Brit's new barn. But Drusilla stood firm, blocking their way.

"There's just one thing," she said innocently. "Brit's barn

needs fixing. And if it ain't fixed, there ain't no food!"

Bumptius Matius raised his eyebrows. He looked sharply at Drusilla, but she stared right back at him. Her eyes were shining with a steely look of determination... the same look that had made her father the Fort Commander.

Bumptius looked down and said nothing. Drusilla turned back to the men, as the delicious aroma of turnip stew wafted up from Brit's open-air kitchen.

"Get Brit's barn fixed, and stack all his harvest safely inside," Drusilla instructed. "Then we can all enjoy a tasty meal together!"

The now-starving soldiers cheered again and got to work straight away. Even Bumptius helped, plotting out the new barn extension with his goma and organising the building of the new walls.

A squad of soldiers brought the rafters
from the old barn and rebuilt the roof.
Brit's new barn was going to be bigger
and better than the old one ever was!

Brit sat happily stirring the stew,
adding a cabbage leaf here and a
handful of barley there.

Searching the hedgerows for apples and blackberries, he found aromatic herbs that made the stew taste and smell even better. The soldiers sniffed and rubbed their stomachs.

"When's supper?" they drooled.

"When the barn is finished!" Drusilla said, firmly.

"But we're so hungry!" they complained.

"Then you'd better get on with it!" Drusilla shouted back.

She picked up a stick and began scratching the grass next to the barn, until a brown, muddy X shape was clearly visible.

"Follow me!" ordered Drusilla, as she led the catapult-firing crew up the hill. She told the remaining soldiers to stand by the grassy X.

At the top of the hill, Drusilla stood by the enormous pile of hay, turnips and cabbages – just where her father had stood earlier in the day.

"I want all of this –" she pointed at the food, "– moved down there." She pointed back down towards the barn, where she had made the X in the grass.

"Ready?" she called. "Aim… fire!"

On her command, a shower of turnips scudded through the air.

"Catch!" Drusilla yelled to the soldiers waiting below.

The soldiers ran about, faces staring skywards, squinting at the rain of turnips heading their way. They jumped, they leapt, they dived and swooped, catching each and every one of the precious turnips.

While the soldiers safely stored the turnips away in the new barn, the catapult was made ready with its next load. Bundles of hay and cabbages came flying down the valley. All were soon stacked away for the winter.

Finally came the sacks of barley, turning head over tail as they gracefully curved across the dazzling yellow sunset.

The soldiers held out their cloaks like nets to catch them. Not a grain was spilled.

CHAPTER FOUR

After much heaving and grumbling from the soldiers, Brit's new home was finally built. His harvest was safely stacked away, and his few belongings arranged neatly by his bed. Everyone was standing outside the barn, on tenterhooks for the meal to be served.

Finally, Brit stopped stirring, and clanged the side of his cooking pot. "Time for supper!" he called. "Come and get it!"

The ravenous soldiers lined up next to Brit's cooking bowl, licking their lips, desperate for a spoonful of stew.

"NOT SO FAST!"

Some of the men looked close to tears as a furious Gluteus Maximus stormed in  between them and the pot. Would they *ever* get any supper?

"I still haven't seen anyone hit a target!" roared the Fort Commander. "You have one last chance. If one of you – just one – can hit a target, then I'll let you eat."

The soldiers looked wearily at one
another. Who would be the one to take
the shot? There was only one more rock
left to shoot. It was all that was left of
Brit's old barn.

Drusilla stepped forward.

"Load the catapult!" she ordered in a
firm, clear voice. "X marks the target!"

The men looked from Drusilla to her
father and back again.

Gluteus Maximus blinked for a moment, before letting out a low chuckle.

"Come on then," he said, smiling proudly at his daughter. "See if you can show them how it's done!"

Brit, Drusilla, Gluteus and the soldiers traipsed up the hill a final time. The men loaded the catapult, and let Drusilla direct them.

"Right, right, ri-i-i-ght!" she called to the crew, pointing with her finger. "Stop! That's too far." She pointed to the left.

"Le-e-e-e-ft, a little bit and… stop!" She screwed up her eyes and lined her aim up on the grassy X below. The light was fading fast.

Drusilla calculated the distance in her head. "Take the strain one more notch."

The catapult crew pulled the firing arm down one more click. As they did, a shooting star whizzed across the darkening skyline.

"Ready, men?" She dropped her hand. "And… FIRE!"

The rock flew through the air and
landed with a great THUD. It buried
itself into the ground, right in the middle
of the X.

Every head turned slowly to face the
Commander. He pursed his lips and
slowly folded his arms. No one said a
word. Slowly, his head began to nod, and
a thin smile crept over his lips.

"Good shot, poppet!" he laughed. "If only everyone in the Roman Army was like you! Okay, men – suppertime!"

The soldiers almost collapsed with joy. They tumbled down the hill to Brit's barn – now fully built and stocked with food. The men took off their helmets and cleaned them out to act as bowls for their well-earned turnip stew.

As the men ate, Gluteus Maximus inspected Brit's new barn, checking everything was stored away neatly and in order.

"See!" he said. "This barn is just as good as the old one. Even better! In fact, I think I've done you a favour, young man!"

Drusilla rolled her eyes.

Brit tried not to laugh. "Yes, Sir," he said. "Thank you very much, Sir!"

CHAPTER FIVE

Later than night, Brit snuggled down
in the sweet-smelling hay. He listened
to the sounds of the night and watched
the huge, orange harvest moon rise up
above the valley. There was just one
more thing to do.

He found his pipes and began playing his special tune. The notes drifted on the dewy air, across the valley and into the still night.

Minutes later, Festus stood in the doorway, panting and wagging his tail.

"It's okay, boy," said Brit. "You can tell the sheep to come back. The soldiers have all gone – there'll be no mutton stew tonight."

Festus barked to the sheep outside. Shyly and timidly, one by one, they came inside and settled down for the night in their new home. Festus lay down next to his master.

"Ah!" Brit put his arm around his faithful dog and yawned. "There'll be no hurry getting up in the morning, Festus. And no more rude awakenings, I hope!"

ROMAN BRIT

COLLECT THEM ALL!

Also available
as an ebook